I'm Going

These levels are meant only as guides;
you and your child can best choose a book that's right.

Level 1: Kindergarten–Grade 1 . . . Ages 4–6

- word bank to highlight new words
- consistent placement of text to promote readability
- easy words and phrases
- simple sentences build to make simple stories
- art and design help new readers decode text

Level 2: Grade 1 . . . Ages 6–7

- word bank to highlight new words
- rhyming texts introduced
- more difficult words, but vocabulary is still limited
- longer sentences and longer stories
- designed for easy readability

Level 3: Grade 2 . . . Ages 7–8

- richer vocabulary of up to 200 different words
- varied sentence structure
- high-interest stories with longer plots
- designed to promote independent reading

Level 4: Grades 3 and up . . . Ages 8 and up

- richer vocabulary of more than 300 different words
- short chapters, multiple stories, or poems
- more complex plots for the newly independent reader
- emphasis on reading for meaning

LEVEL 1

Library of Congress Cataloging-in-Publication Data Available

2 4 6 8 10 9 7 5 3 1

Published by Sterling Publishing Co., Inc.
387 Park Avenue South, New York, NY 10016
Text copyright © 2006 by Harriet Ziefert Inc.
Illustrations copyright © 2006 by Laura Rader
Distributed in Canada by Sterling Publishing
c/o Canadian Manda Group, 165 Dufferin Street
Toronto, Ontario, Canada M6K 3H6
Distributed in Great Britain and Europe by Chris Lloyd at Orca Book
Services, Stanley House, Fleets Lane, Poole BH15 3AJ, England
Distributed in Australia by Capricorn Link (Australia) Pty. Ltd.
P.O. Box 704, Windsor, NSW 2756, Australia

I'm Going To Read is a trademark of Sterling Publishing Co., Inc.

Printed in China

Sterling ISBN 13: 978-1-4027-3075-7
Sterling ISBN 10: 1-4027-3075-6

For information about custom editions, special sales, premium and
corporate purchases, please contact Sterling Special Sales
Department at 800-805-5489 or specialsales@sterlingpub.com.

Grow Little Turnip, Grow Big

Pictures by Laura Rader

Sterling Publishing Co., Inc.
New York

An old man planted
a little turnip.

the big

"Grow little turnip, grow big,"
said the old man.

One day the old man
went to pull the turnip up.

He pulled and pulled.
But he could not pull it up.

hoo!

He called
the old woman.

The old woman pulled the old man.
The old man pulled the turnip.

They pulled and pulled.
But they could not pull it up.

Yoo

The old woman called
the little girl.

hoo!

The little girl pulled the old woman.
The old woman pulled the old man.

The old man pulled the turnip.
They pulled and pulled.
But they could not pull it up.

Yoo

The little girl called
the big dog.

The big dog pulled the girl.
The girl pulled the old woman.
The old woman pulled the old man.

The old man pulled the turnip.
They pulled and pulled.
But they could not pull it up.

The dog called
the cat.

The cat pulled the dog.
The dog pulled the girl.
The girl pulled the old woman.
The old woman pulled the old man.
The old man pulled the turnip.

They pulled and pulled.
But they could not pull it up.

The cat called
the tiny mouse.

The mouse pulled the cat.
The cat pulled the dog.
The dog pulled the girl.

The girl pulled the old woman.
The old woman pulled the old man.
The old man pulled the turnip.

They pulled and
pulled and pulled.
And out came . . .

the turnip!